P9-CQL-028

Life SUCKS

Life SUCKS

Jessica ABEL Gabe SORIA Warren PLEECE

Color by Hilary Sycamore

First Second

... Gino Michelini on KLS-FM, 92.3 on your FM dial! For those of you heading home on another fine and smoggy LA evening, I got good news and I got bad news. The good news is you're goin' home. The bad news is it's gonna take awhile. Let's get the traffic rundown from Lisa Neville. Lisa?
Click!
6:30 PM

Thanks, Gino. From up here in the sky, it's bumper to bumper on the 134 from the 2 to the 210. If you're headed home on the Santa Monica, expect a big wait westbound due to an overturned cantaloupe truck at La Brea. On the 110 ...
PM

6:30

S'up, carl?
"Morning," Dave.

DAVE'S

What's on?
El Amor de los Amores.

Cool. Did Lupe kill herself, or what?
Not yet.

You know she's gonna.
Not while Esteban is still out there.

You going to work?
Ughhhh ...

Thanks for reminding me, "Dad."

WASTE

Dave, my man, just in time! If my ass isn't on my couch in twenty-five minutes, my parole officer is gonna be wicked pissed.
Last Stop

Sorry, dude. When do you get that thing off again?

Six months, man, then it's no more random piss tests!

I totally paid for this, man.
Yeah, whatever. What're you gonna do then?

Then I'm Mexico bound, amigo!
That's cool.

I'll only be here for all eternity.

Oh, by the way, call Radu! Later, dude!

Brïïnnng!!
And so it begins.

Last Stop, service 24-7, how can I help you?

Radu, I was just going to call you.
Right, right. "Lord Arisztidescu," sorry, my lord.

Yes, the hot dogs have been rotated. Yes, already.
No, I haven't counted out the register yet.

I totally paid for this.
No, the day guy didn't take anything.

Yes, I'll call you when I count it out.
No, I have to install the pork cracklins display tonight.

OK, I'll talk to you later, sir.

lboro

lboro

You do double coupons?

What are the odds on this week's Lotto?

Adult diapers?

lboro

Frito
Dorit

This jerky tastes funny! I wanna refund!

A refund? You didn't even **buy** it!

I'm never shopping here again!
ATM
HERE

Are you even listening to me?

Dave!
Hellooo!?

Jerome.
You'll be hearing from my lawyers!

Look at the time!
I never should have told you about it. I should have known you'd turn it into some stupid "event."

Whaddya mean you shouldna told me?! Aren't I your best friend?
No, Carl is my best friend.

Yeah, well, anyway, so then we need bonding experiences! Like the Running of the Goths!
"The Running ..."

Jerome, it's just closing time at the juice bar.
A majestic sight, isn't it?

I can't believe you just up and closed your shop. Aren't you the only one on at this hour?
Yeah, but Vlad trusts me; he's pretty hands-off.

That's because Wes didn't used to work at Kwik Kopy. You lucky bastard.
You seen the Wesster lately?

No, thank God! He's made himself scarce lately. I heard he's got some new love slave keepin' him busy.
Oooh, **love** slave!

Shut up! Here they come.

For girls obsessed with lying in the cold embrace of Death, they're pretty damn hot!

How about that one? Woo-eee!

You don't even **know**. Wait till you see her.
Pfft. How different could she be?

But, realistically, you know, I'd do most of 'em.

Hell, I'd even do that fat one.

Crap. Keep your eye out, man. She's got long black hair.

Um ...

Oh, wait, I gotta grab something else ...
Nachos

Okay, root beer...
Root beer!

Two orders of nachos ...
Nachos?!
That'll be $3.97.

You people eat nachos?! That's like the most **unscary** food ever!
Bite me.

Where do you want it?

Man, you're sooo lucky! You have a whole juice bar full of nubile death-rocking maidens in your strip mall, and all I get at this time of night are the old ladies with the "cat missing" posters ...
Shut up, man!

... and old geezers making religious pamphlets!
Jerome, shut up! It's her! And she's ...

... **coming in** ...
OPEN

... Yeah, he's totally beautiful. His cloak was **so** elegant.
I know, can you believe it? He designed it himself. And those boots ...

I **know!!**

I heard that the guy who does the fangs for **Buffy** did his.
Wow, those things must cost more than I make in a month.

He gave me a black orchid. I mean ...
You are **so** lucky.

Yeah, I know.

Oh, see, here it is, "blood-orange juice." Imported from Italy. Isn't that cool?
And you can get it at the Last Stop??
I **know!!**
Explosion

I heard it has more vitamins.
Ding-a-ling!
Dave! Look! Get a load of **this** jackass.

Ah, my dark princess. I crave sustenance.

You want some blood-orange juice?
SANGUINELLA
explosion

I don't drink ... orange juice.

Mmm, perhaps, but first offer me your lovely throat.
Alistair, not in the store!

Hee hee hee ... ow! Alistair!

You GUYS! I thought "vampires" didn't have sex! Especially not in the Last Stop!

Allow me to purchase this for you, my queen.
Will this be all?

Yes, yes! Did I present you with any other item? Ring this up, peon. The night grows short.
Alistair!

Sorry, sir.
Peon is a perfectly accurate word for a serving person.

"Sir"?
I don't care. It's rude. You guys go wait outside, I'll buy this.

Very well. But don't tarry too long, my dear. I need to have a blood feed tonight. I hunger for steak! RARE!
Gross!

I wish he was a vegetarian.
I wish I was a vegetarian.

You should try it! It's easier than you think.
Yeah, well, there are some things I just can't give up.

Here's your change. Have a nice night.
Bye!
Bye! Come again!

Wow, you're right, she **is** hot.
Back off, man. I saw her first.

Re-lax, Dave. You planted the seed, and I'm not going to harvest your crops, man! But can you believe that Eddie Munster-wannabe dork?

I'm gonna kill myself.
That'd be way too much work. And in the end, whaddya got? You're dead and the chump still has the girl. Instead, whyncha just kill him?

Oh, it's just **that** easy, is it?

Yeah, just get him in a dark alley, rip out his carotid, and get the blood flowing! It'd be an appropriate death, right? He might even be happy!
Uuch. Just talking about it makes me queasy.

You and your blood thing, man. Look, I'll take him out, OK? You don't have to get your hands bloody.
Jerome ...

OK, OK! I'm sorry I said the **B** word! But hey, I'll do him for you, just on general principle. I know you like the girl, but that guy's a tool. I'd be doing the world a favor.
Right, whatever.

Dave's the king of the nighttime world, and she's! Dave's! midnight queen!

Jerome, you're depressing me. If there's one thing that I am **not**, it's the king of the nighttime world ... Man, I'm not even 100th in line for the throne. Dracula, Radu, even that girl's boyfriend, Count Spazula, comes in before me.

Dave, my friend, there's no way I could make you feel worse than you do yourself.
Right, sure. So tell me. What've I got that that guy doesn't got?

Let's see ... He doesn't have an **awesome** job at the Last Stop!
Ha ha. Funny.

You're a suave "older gentleman."
Who'll get carded for the rest of my miserable existence.

You've got, um ...

... a better wardrobe?
Nice try.

C'mon now, buck up, little camper! Who are the real vampires around here, him or us?

We are.
That's right, Davey-wavey. We are.

At least you enjoy it.

I just roll with the changes, my friend. Pass me a can of goth broth, yeah? I need a pick-me-up before I head back to work.
Unlife blows. I'm just going to go out to the beach and wait for sunrise. You can pay your respects at the black spot on Zuma Beach.

Heck, there isn't anybody here. Let's take in the air.
I gotta rotate the hot dogs, Jerome.
Stop

Screw the hot dogs!

Ding-a-ling!
Hey!

What's your problem, man?

You can't go outside with an open container!
... of blood?

Especially of blood, dimwit.
Last Stop

Nice night.

Yeah. Real dark.

Aw, crap. Is that who I think it is?

It's Radu. Checking up on me. Look busy.
Be cool, man.

Cherome, you creemeenal! Deed you pay for zat beer?

Sheesh, Radu, man, I was just about to!

Hey!
Yoink!

You are going to ruin me, Dave. You geeve my money away!
Uh, change?

And you, Cherome, cheating my friend Vlad! Hees shop iss closed! Vhere are za people to make copies?

Oh, man, you're right. Look at the time! My break's just about over! Dave, man, gotta fly!

Hey, Radu ...
Yes?

Bite me!

You leettle ... leettle ...
Sonova ...

Vhat iss za vurd, Dave?
Punk.

Punk! Yes! Now come viss me, Dave.

Yes, Master.

Dave, Dave, Dave ... vhat am I to do viss you? I give you geeft of eternal life, I promote you to assistant manager, and zis iss how you repay? By not punching out on break?
How do you know I didn't punch out?

A vampire master knows such sings about hees childe, Dave.

For instance, I also know zat you have not rotated hot dogs.
I was just about to!

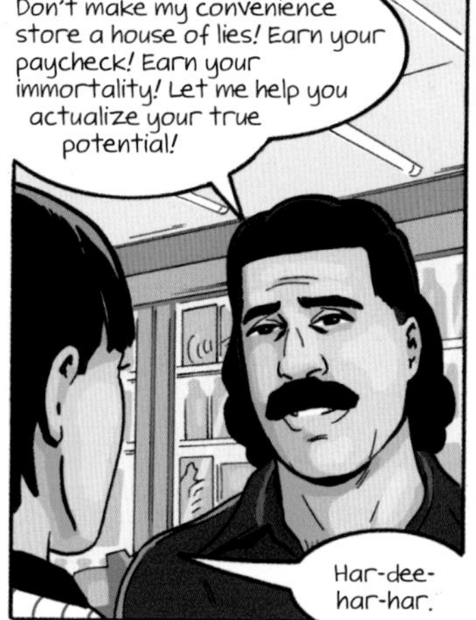
Don't make my convenience store a house of lies! Earn your paycheck! Earn your immortality! Let me help you actualize your true potential!
Har-dee-har-har.

Har-dee ...?
Are you contradicting me, my childe? Vould you like to leave my employment? You know zere's only one vay to quit, and it's ... messy.

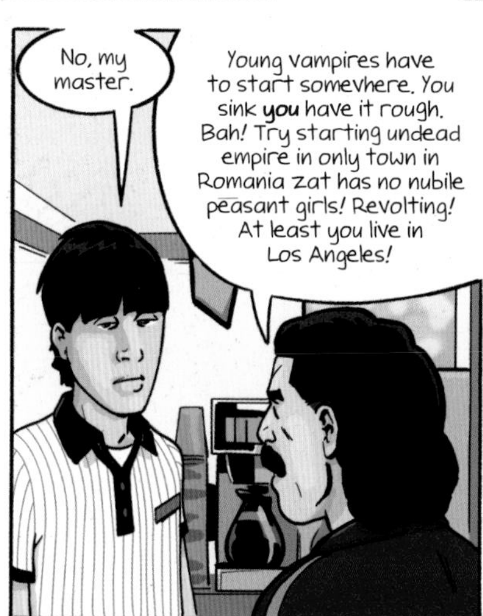
No, my master.
Young vampires have to start somevhere. You sink **you** have it rough. Bah! Try starting undead empire in only town in Romania zat has no nubile peasant girls! Revolting! At least you live in Los Angeles!

As young vampire in Romania, I shoveled bullshit for feefteen years!

Zat's right! And bulls make lot of shit! I know from experience! You do vhat you have ...

Two years previous ...
Ding-a-ling!
Help Wanted
ATM
Excuse me ...
No ID, no beer. Vill sell cigarettes, though.
Oh no, sir, I'm just looking for the owner.
For vhat for you look for za owner?
Uh, Help Wanted ...
Ah! It iss fortunate zen, iss it not, zat I am za owner?
You vurk nights no problem?
Yes, sir. In fact, I'm looking for a night job. I'm starting school next month during the day. Community college.
Ah, young man who vants education. Very ambitious! But your ... parents do not pay for you?
Unfortunately not. That'd be nice, but I'm all on my own on this one.
Impressive vurk ethic. You vurk hard, yes?
Totally! I mean, yes, sir, Mr ...?
Staff Only
Arisztidescu. Lord Radu Arisztidescu. And you are ...?
Dave Miller, sir, er, I mean, your highness ...

Tch! Iss nossing. Title iss relic from Olde Country. Zis **America,** land of equal stuff. You, me, vee vill be friends. Covurkers. **Team members.**
"Team members?" You mean ...
Yes. I like you. I geeve you good job.
Don't you even want me to fill out an application? Check my references?
Dave!
I need nossing but my Olde Romanian intueetion. And it tells me ...
Tells you what?
Zat you should help bring case of Yoo Hoo from za storeroom, my new ... **employee.**
Wow, that was the easiest job interview ever!
Blah ha ha ha!
So, how much do I get per hou-ow-ow-ow-ow OOOOOOOWWWW!
Blah ha ha ha!

How iss it possible? Vell, let me tell you. Vampire must not only be scary ...

... but have good head for business.
Who invested his entire fortune in Pets dot com?

I heard zat! Ungrateful wretch! Get back to vurk! Sveep parking lot. Iss filthy!

The parking lot?! But ...

Blah ha ha ha!

I go now to play cards at za Lodge. Sveep, boy, sveep! And don't forget to rotate hot dogs!

Pet store on Internet **still** good idea ...
Rotate this, you cheap bastard ...

At least tomorrow's my day off ...

Dave!
Yo, Dave! Wake up!

Huh? Turnoutdalight ... sleepin'.

You got a phone call, man.
Whoever it is, tell 'em I'm dead.

He knows that already. It's Radu.
Aw crap, what does he want?

What **time** is it, anyway?
Seven.
S'early! Why am I awake?

Hello?
"Hello" **vhat**?

Geez ... "Hel-LO, Master, what is your bidding?"
Zat's more like it!

What's up?
I am needing you to come to vurk.

Come to ...? Radu! It's my day off! What happened to Mouktar??
Vell, you know ...

No, I **don't** know.
Mouktar isn't here. Technically.

Oh, God, not again ...
He vas late, Dave! And I hadn't had lunch. You know how cranky I get vhen I'm hungry!

Radu! Mouktar was awesome! Honest, hard-working, willing to work nights!
Vhat can I say? Anyhow, you must vurk Mouktar's shift.

No way!
I **command** it.
Urgh! Yes, Master.

Crunch!

It's so **weird** that you have a "master"!

VA-VA-VA-VROOOOOM!!
BEEP BEEP!

Whuh!

What the hell??

The Davester! Lookin' sharp!
Wes! What the hell was that?!

Just havin' fun, amigo! Enjoying my new ride.

Ain't your "amigo."
Touchy!

Oh, man, my bike! Look what you did to it!
Dude, I didn't touch your bike!

Dude, you totally should see the look on your face right now!
Oh, forget it.

No problem. I'll give you a ride. You seen my new car yet?
I'd rather walk.

Check it out! Six cylinders, 240 horsepower, tinted windows ...
So, where can I take ya?
I could give a rat's ass ...

Don't worry about it, you've done me enough favors for today.
Seriously, Dave, what crawled up your butt? If it's about your bike ...

Aaargh!

When are you going to get it! I'm not your "amigo," pal. See this shirt? See this uniform? *You* are the reason for this uniform.

See these teeth? **YOU** are the reason for these teeth!

Don't point the finger at me! I didn't make you.
Yeah, but if you weren't so useless, Radu wouldn't have needed to make a new night manager!

Hey, man, take that up with Radu! A convenience store? Me? I mean, seriously, bro.
I'm not your brother either!

Hey, you know, two vamps, same master ... kinda!
Don't make me sick.

Fine, then screw you! You can walk to work!
Thank you.

... and, as you can see, I couldn't ride my bike.
Vell, I have to dock you for time you are late, iss policy. But, vhere Vess iss, iss trouble. Iss not your fault.

Zere. Vill vurk.

Weellll ... I guess it should be good enough to get home on.
Hmph. Of course. Vhat do you say?

Uh ... thanks, Radu. I appreciate it.
Iss nothing. Happy vurker iss good vurker, Dave. Like I always say.

You never say that.

I say always from now. Now get to vurk. Ice cream sandvich need stocking.
I'm on it.

Ding-a-ling

Peace, boss man.
You're fifteen minutes late! You can't be late! Late is not cool.

Chill out, man. I'm here, aren't I? You can't be a slave to the clock, Dave. It ain't healthy.

Whatever ... Look, I started the morning coffee for you, and the inventory sheets are ready to go. The delivery guy should be here in about half an hour. Check the dates on the milk!

Oh, hey, man, is that your bike parked outside?
Yeah.

Gnarly. Somebody stole your handlebars.

Last Stop
Last St

How am I gonna get home in time?!
Dude, what's the hassle? Just take the bus home.
LACC

Screw the bus! You know how long that takes? I **have** to be home by 6:26.
Whoa.

I gotta go.

Guess Mr. Fancy Assistant Manager thinks he's too good for the bus.

Precious, what's wrong?

Sweetie-baby, what's the matter?

Oh, man!

Oh my God. Come back! Sit! Stay!

Man, are you OK?

They don't bite! I swear! Heel! Heel! Bad dog!

Wow, this is a new one.

Whoa!

Sheesh. This day is going to kill me one way or another.

6:22??

Hey.

Heeeeey ... um, Last Stop guy, right?

Right. Say, do you think I could trouble you for a ride?

You're sure you're not a knife-wielding psycho maniac?

OK, sure. Get in.
LASC

I've gotta get home before 6:26. It's a matter of life or death.

Oh yeah? What happens at 6:26?

If I don't get home before then I'll burst into fla ...

Uh, I'll miss the repeat of **El Amor de los Amores**. It's on at 6:30. I've gotta see if Lupe is finally going to commit suicide.
I, uh, missed it last night!

You watch that corny stuff? I mean, don't take this the wrong way, but you seem a little, um ...
What?

White? Geeky? A dorky gringo like me can't like **El Amor de los Amores**?
Nooo ... It's just that it's my **mom's** favorite show.

Take a right.

Hey, whatever.

Oh my God, is that the sun??

Cuz, uh, the sun comes up at 6:26 ... We gotta hurry!

Uh ... huh.

Cuz, uh, I, uh ... I gotta pee first!
Relax, I'll get you there.

It's up here on the right.

Riiiiight HERE! Stop!
I hope this episode is worth it.

Yep, sure is! Look, I can't talk right now, but thanks for the ride. I owe you big time.

You're welcome. Velasquez Chauffeur Service always at the ready.

I can't believe Lupe nasn't committed suicide yet.

Ow, ow, ow!

What're you doing out so late? You're usually home way before sunrise.
Some clown stole my handlebars. I seriously thought I wasn't going to make it home. But I got a ride. From a girl I met at the Last Stop.

Oh yeah? What's her name?
!

I knew there was something I was forgetting!

Oh man, Carl, you hould see her ... She is oo beautiful. And she's nice, too. Man, she's **perfect**.
Except for the fact that she's still breathing and you are the working undead.
There is that.

Dude, change the channel. **El Amor de los Amores** is on.
Oh yeah, sorry.

Later ...
12:13 pm

Can't sleep, huh?

Not a wink.

The girl?
Yep.

Damn. She must be pretty cute.
Carl, you have no idea.

So what's up? We gonna find her or what?

Last Stop
Tax 'n' Stuff
TAX PREP
immigracion
ABOGADO TO GO
99¢ STORE

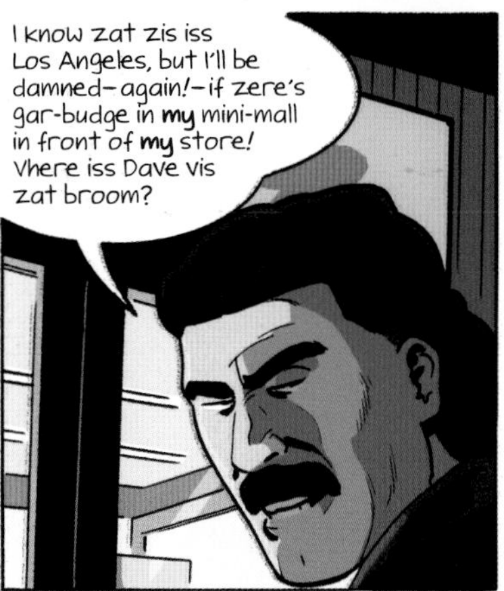
I know zat zis iss Los Angeles, but I'll be damned—again!—if zere's gar-budge in **my** mini-mall in front of **my** store! Vhere iss Dave vis zat broom?

Eh? Vhat zis? Taking paid breaks **again,** no doubt. Lazy, no-good American vampires ...

Ding-a-ling!
Dave! Dave, vhere are you, you lazy vhelp? Vhy have you left my precious store unattended?

Help ...
Eh?

My GOD ...

Help.
I've been
shot...
Vhat
happened to za
money, Dave?!
Coffee
Corner

Get up. Get up! Vhat are you doing on za floor? Did you punch out for zis "break"?

Radu ... a guy came ... shot me.
With a gun.
I'm sorry ... about the cash ... but need ... doctor ...

Dave, must I remind you zat you are a vampire? A supernatural creature of great strength and cunning?

You do not need a doctor. You need to get up off of za floor!
OW!

Ach, such a crying baby! If you vould only hunt and drink human blood like normal vampire, zen vee vouldn't be having zis talk! You vould be feasting on za scoundrel who dared rob me, Lord Radu Arisztidescu!
But ...

Nonsense! All-plasma diet leaves you veak as kitten. Disgraceful!

Ding-a-ling!
Wassup, Dave. Hey, Radu. I mean, Lord Arisztidescu. You wouldn't believe the luck I just had ...

Ooooh!
Dave! Don't faint! You are such ... such ... Cherome,
Vhat is vurd?

Wuss?
You are such vooss! Get **up**! Ach! Cherome! Now I have to ... I am forced ... Cherome, lock door and put sign up!

So, vhat in Vlad's name iss going on vis you two boys!?
LAST STOP: WE'LL BE BACK REAL FAST!

... Iss not for nossing I have vampire for night manager! Iss part of business plan! Convenience store night shift very dangerous for mortal. At Last Stop iss dangerous for **creemeenal**!

Look: I'm sorry I'm not a bloodthirsty maniac like Jerome.
Hey, listen, Dave. This was a **bad** guy. Definitely. I was providing community service! I mean, look at all this cash he had. I think he must have been a big drug dealer.

Or he could have just cashed his paycheck!
Bad guy, cashed paycheck, who cares! Dave, you must eat! And Cherome, I applaud your culinary instinct, but you are so sloppy!

Yeah, I know, but, like, the guy moved, and like I sort of bit his neck like, all open and stuff! He was like a fire hydrant!
Uuuuuugh!

Sorry, dude. Too graphic.
Don't be sorry. He iss vooss. Cherome, you must practice biting technique. Zat iss it. Keep up good vurk.

Now, Dave. Vhat's happening?
OK, well ...

The guy barged in and barely looked at me before he pulled out a gun and shot me! He grabbed the cash, and a pack of Ding-Dongs, and booked. That's it.

Ding-Dongs? What did this guy look like? Cuz, like, my guy, he had Ding-Dongs.
Red sweatband on his head?
Yeah!
Poodle mullet?
UH huh!
Sky blue jogging suit?
Yeah, man, that was totally my guy!

Cherome! You are hero! You are saving my money!
Yoink!

But ...
No "buts," you are hero.

Here iss reward.
Five bucks ...?

And my eternal gratitude. Coming from vampire, zat actually **means** somesing.
I **guess**.

And take a Blood Brew on me. Who says I am cheap?

He has promise, zat one. Maybe someday vee invite him to join club.

Suck up.
Watch it– bloodsucker humor!

Ah, man! *You* know what my problem is? I've been hanging out with too many goddamned vampires!
Dave, get a new shirt back here and open store! I am tired of losing money!
Coffee Corner

Later...
God, what a dork. At least the bullet holes and blood on the old one made it look vaguely cool.
You trying to impress somebody? In that getup?

Keep dreaming, buddy.
...

Oh my God, you **are**! You wanna look cool just in case that hot Goth chick comes in again!
Yeah, right! I'm perfectly aware that ...

Oh-ho! My boy's trying to get his mack on. And perhaps then get his snack on?
No way!

OK, look, I ... I can't stop thinking about her, man. Ever since that morning when she saved my bacon from frying, she's all that's been on my mind.

It's crazy, I know, but I think I'm falling in love with her.
LOVE?! You just met her!

Oh, man. A vampire pinin' away for a mortal. How pathetically Anne Rice can you get?
I know it's lame!

... I just ... it's just... I feel it, that's all.

Fag.

OK! OK! Seriously. I am not unsympathtic to your plight. I wanna help you out. But how?

I got it!

No, that's not it.

Brilliant!

Nah, that'll get us arrested. At LEAST.

Ah ...! No, that's what the Three Stooges would do.
Will you cut it out?

Funny ... I don't hear any brilliant strategies coming out of YOUR mouth.
Likewise.

Ding-a-ling!
Dude! Is that ...?

Yeah, it's **her** friend.
Well, there you go, Dave. Ask her about your girlie when she pays for her stuff!

You think?
Yeah, I think! Here she comes!

You guys don't carry **Today's Darkness**, do you?
What?

Today's Darkness. It's a magazine.
Uh, no.

Oh, OK. Thanks anyway.

Ask her, you moron!
What do I **say**?

Maaaaan ...
Step back and watch the master handle this.

Excuse me, miss?

Yes?

Look into my eyes. COME to Jerome.

Jerome! What the hell are you doing?
Vampire hypnotism, my friend. Badass, huh?

Yes, my master?
Isn't that freaking **awesome**?

Hey, don't argue with results.

You came in here with a friend last week, did you not, my darling?
Yessssss ...

My friend here has an embarrassing schoolboy crush on your friend, but he was too much of a chickenshit to ask you about her.
Hee-hee!
Hey!

So tell me, tell me, my delicate night flower: How can my friend "hook up" with the sweet young thing? What is her name? Where can she be found?
Her name's Rosa. And, well ... he could try to find her ... at work?

Yes? Work? Where, my child?
At ... Diva's Dungeon. She works ... tomorrow night.

Excellent. Be free of my spell, now.
... But never forget how attractive you find me.

Uh ... What was I asking?

Sorry, miss, we don't carry **Today's Darkness**. Try Hollywood News and Periodicals up the street.
Right ... thanks.

See ya later, cutie.

I gotta admit, that WAS pretty awesome.

You, too, can have amazing, fantastical vampire powers if you drink your blood, son. Better than X-Ray Spex, man.

The Next Evening ...
So what the heck is a "Diva's Dungeon," anyway?
lemon Sunrise
TROY

Their ad in the **Weekly** says that they sell "Fetish gear, punk shirts, and stuff that defies description."

Sounds kinda scary.

"Sounds kinda scary," he says. Dave, you're such a pansy.

It pains me to agree with Jerome, but he's right; what kind of bloodsucker worries about "scary" lingerie stores?
What do you know about bloodsucking, puny human?

More than **you** know about it, Mr. "I Only Drink Plasma" vampire vegetarian.
Oh, SNAP!

Hey! There's the store.
And there's a parking space.
Whoo! Rock Star Parking!

So, how do I look?

Like a dork.
Like some kind of jerk.
All right, then. Let's go.

But ... what if she doesn't like me?
Dave, shut up and go in.

ell, duh. What do you mean
hat if" she doesn't like
ou? You'll probably have to
y out some vampire
hypnotism.

You're psyched. You're totally psyched. You're not a loser.

Who the hell am I kidding?

Can I help you find anything?
I don't know. Do you have any ...

It's **you!** Weird Mexican-soap-opera guy. I mean, um ...
Hey! Oh, hey! What's going on?

Rosa.
Dave, actually.

Yeah. Pleasure to meet you.
Again.

Yeah. Again.
Sooooo ...
Yeah.

How did everything turn out on **El Amor de los Amores**? Lupe kill herself yet?
No. She wimped out yet again.

Again?! Hasn't she been threatening to do it for, like, six months?
Pretty much. I figure that someday soon Ramon's gonna get sick of these false alarms and take care of her himself.

You know what I mean?
Ha ha ha ha! That's morbid.

Hey, just cuz a guy doesn't wear leather pants or pirate shirts or whatever doesn't mean he's a square.
I didn't mean anything by it. It's just that you look kind of ... out of place in here.

Hey, I'm cool. I'm in the market for, uh ...

Something just like that.

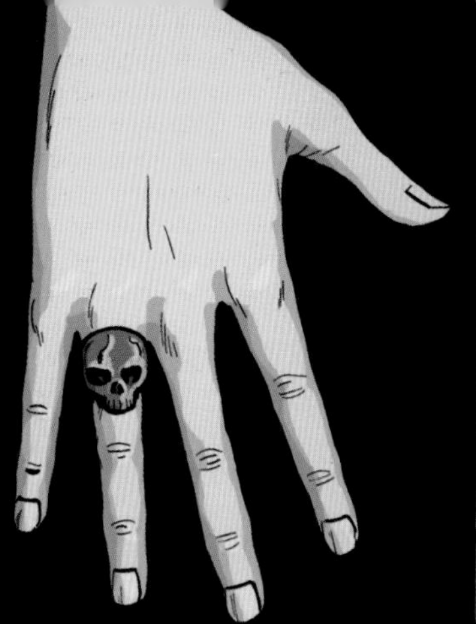

You? Bought **this**? Dave, I'm stunned.
Looks pretty cool.

And that's $5.50 back to you.
Who're your friends?
Oh! Carl and Jerome, this is Rosa. Rosa, this is my roommate Carl and my, uh, work associate Jerome.

Hey. Nice to meetcha.
All mine.
Hey.

So, we have to get going.
Already?
Gotta work. You know how it is.

Tell me about it. Hey, I'll be at the club later tonight – I'll drop in and say hi, OK?
Oh, uh, that'd be great! Uh, see you then! C'mon, pardners. Let's hit the trail. Bye, Rosa.

Bye, Dave. Nice to meet you, Jerome and Carl.

Crunch!
Yes!
Hey!

Sorry ...

Just got a little excited there.
Don't worry about it, Carl. Nothing a little Bondo won't fix.

The next time you get all excited about a girl, take it out on yourself, not my car, OK?

Geez. I didn't even know I could **do** that.

Later that evening at the Last Stop ...
Ahhhhh, sugar ... duh duh DUH duh duh duh ... ah, honey, honey ... duh duh DUH duh duh duh— you are my can-dy giiiiirl ...

... And you got me wantin' you!
Ding-a-ling!

Rosa!

Duuuude! What's shakin', bacon?
Hello, Wes.

Hey, listen, amigo, I'm havin' some people over, and, I see you're working, so, sorry you can't come, but I need to lay in some supplies.
OK, go shop, I'll be here!

No, I mean, look, I'm having **people** over. I need five cases of beer, and two cases of Blood Brew ...
OK, right on it!

No, no, then I need two handles of bourbon, and ...

Ten minutes later ...
Last

So, that's it! You're all set! See you later!
Dude, relax, I've still gotta pay!

You're gonna **pay**?
Well, you know. Put it on my tab and stuff. Unless Radu went and made everything free.

Oh, right, uh, that's cool. Hey, just sign this slip here, and I'll write it up later...
Ha ha! Dave, man, I know you're an honest dude, but no way am I signing a blank receipt!

Oh, OK.
Man, you're in a hurry.

I've never gotten fast service from you before! What's the ...
DIRGE

Hey, Dave, working hard, huh?
Ah hah! **Cherchez la femme!**
Ah, nuts.

Hey, Rosa. You look great.
Oh, thanks, I just finished smocking this yoke tonight.
Huh?
DIRGE

Sewing the dress.
Oh, you made it? Wow, that's cool.

Yeah. Verrrry sexy. Wes likes.
Excuse me?

I like it. I like the whole thing. The girly-girl look.

Wes Hardy. We've got a mutual frien in Dave here, it seems.

I don't think so.
Wes is more of a business acquaintance, Rosa. He's a regular customer.

C'mon, Dave! Don't be shy! Tell the little lady about our mutual hobbies. She seems like the type who'd really like our scene ...
Uh, no she wouldn't! I mean, **what** mutual hobbies?

I don't think I'd be interested in anything that has to do with **you**.

Dave, I have to get to the club. I'll come back later when your ... company isn't here.
Suit yourself, mamacita. You'll come around.

What did you say?
Nada, nada.

Oh, Dave, by the way, I meant to ask, are you working tomorrow night?
Huh? Uh, no. Why?

... Because there's a fashion show at Dirge. I've got a piece in the show and I'd love it if you'd come. And bring Jerome and Carl, of course.
Oh, uh, great, yeah! Congratulations!

It's at eight o'clock.
But how do I dress?
Oh, don't worry about it. You have a black T-shirt, right?

Sure, yeah.
OK, see you tomorrow, Dave. I have to go meet Alistair.

Hey, see ya later, baby!

OW! Dave! Look at the way she's shaking it. She's gonna look back. She is. Wait for it ... wait ...

There! You see that? Her mind's saying "Hell no," but her body's saying "Oh yeah!"
She could've been looking at me.

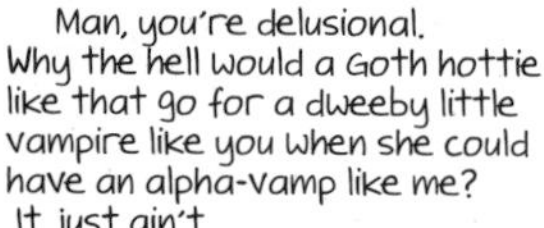
Man, you're delusional. Why the hell would a Goth hottie like that go for a dweeby little vampire like you when she could have an alpha-vamp like me? It just ain't logical.

She's not like that.
You bet she is.
I bet she isn't.

Hey, hey! And here I thought you were the shy retiring type.
Forget it. Here. Sign this.

What? You think you have a chance with her? That's the funniest thing I've heard in days.
Vrrr-ooom!
Screeech

Yee-hah! Dave! Amigo! What the hell is happening?
Jesus, Merle! You almost gave me a heart attack.

What's this jackass doing here taking up my parking space? He bothering you?
No, he was just taking off. Weren't you, Wes?

I've got places to be.

Hyaah!
Heh-heh. See ya, guys.

I really, really hate spoiled, rich-boy vampires. They make my blood boil.

How about a tallboy of Blood Brew on the house, Merle?
Right on, my man. Right on.

Whatcha carrying that guy's groceries for? Ain't you got less important things to do?
Radu's been reading too many management self-help books lately ...

And you gotta do what Radu says.
Well, actually, yeah.

Oh, and I need two six-packs of Blood Bitter and a couple of Clot Jerkies.

Dave? You mind if I give you some advice?
Can I stop you?
Ha ha.

This whole Radu situation ... it blows, man.
Tell me about it.

Him and all his buddies, those broke-ass, ancient vampire-types making young guys like you and Jerome their bloodsucking wage slaves ... That's just low-down. Those guys have not got an ounce of class.

Yeah, but what are you gonna do?

Be a man! Kick their moldy asses! Look at me—living the free and easy life. Riding, nibbling on the maidens, being my own man.
Yeah, but that means your master's dead, right? What happened, a prehistoric Buffy take him out?

Hell no! I'm a Do-It-Yourselfer! I iced that prick back in 1879. Never been happier. I'm not suggesting you should take Radu out, but hell, man, show a little backbone!
How much I owe ya?
$26.50.

Gotta saddle up. Got a **nice** little mortal chick waiting back at my pad. Ooo-wee, you should see this little girl!

Enjoy yourself, Merle. Thanks for the advice.

Anytime, brother. Take it sleazy, Dave.
Later.
ATM

Next evening ...
Dave, your obsession with this chick is really taking us some weird places and opening up new vistas of experience.
Seriously.
DIRGE
Cashing
Freaky Couture Exhibition
TONIGHT!!!

The fashion show hasn't started yet, has it?
The couture Exhibition begins in five minutes.

Thanks, Sandman.
Hmmmph.
Poseurs.

Gah! I'm the poseur? Look at this place! It's like the Junior Prom of Darkness.
Where's the bar? I'm thirsty.
It says here that Rosa's dress is halfway through the show.

Can you imagine if real vampires dressed that way? They'd get beat up by frat boys every day!

Whiskey and soda.
We don't serve alcohol. Juice bar.
SLAYER

This is some stereotypin' bullshit.
Yeah, I mean, we're not **all** Transylvanian!
And, man, those of us who are ...
... if they could only **see** Radu's wardrobe.

Oh. Uh, right.
Geez. What do you recommend?
DIRGE
I see you as the Dragon's Blood type.

You see Rosa anywhere?
She's probably backstage. But her ball and chain's over there with the rest of the Addams Family.

Carrot/ beet/ orange.
Oh ... OK, I'm game.
SLAYER

She invited me when she knew he'd be here? That's not cool.
Man, chicks do that **all the time!**
I'm just some guy to her.

That'll be $8.
Whoa.

Can I get you anything?
Yes. I'd like to buy everybody in the house a sense of humor and a better wardrobe.

What do you think those guys would do if they met a **real** vampire?
Well, if the real vampire was our boy Dave, they'd buy a lottery ticket and two ninety-nine-cent hot dogs from him.
SLAYE
But seriously. I mean, these guys have no idea. Remember, Dave, the day you were made?
Don't bring it up.
Oh, **do** tell!
BRAVO!
It was crazy. I was sitting on the couch in the apartment, watching cartoons, when Dave came in looking like utter crap ...
Damn, Dave. It's six in the morning. You drunk?
I don't feel so good ...
You told me the whole story ...
... and then Radu told me I had to be his blood-drinking, immortal wage slave, working the night shift six days a week.
That is the most fucked-up thing I've ever heard.
I did some scientific tests to determine the extent of his undead vulnerabilities ...
Man, what a beautiful morning.
Close the curtain! CLOSE THE DAMN CURTAIN!
You're joking.
I'll never be tan again.

Ugh, I'm starving!
Have some cereal?
MMM!
Bleurgh! God! It tastes like I just licked an ashtray!
But you love Cocoa Honey Blasts!
Not anymore I don't. Radu didn't tell me this part.
God! I'm hungry.
Don't look at me!!
What am I gonna do? Radu told me to go to this place and get some bags of blood for the fridge, but I was like, screw that! I'm getting some cereal!
I'll go.
No way! I can't let this happen to you! I have no idea who ...
Man, you've been my friend for fifteen years. You're in need. Anyway, it's daylight. No vamp is gonna jump out and get me.

Thanks. I'm just gonna ... sit here.
Anyway, at least now you've got a job and can make rent!

Awww. Isn't that **heartwarming**? You guys should have your own sitcom!
What could I do? He was my only friend in junior high!
Shhh. That's Rosa's dress.

Whoa! That's **Rosa!**

... and here's a divine corset and dress ensemble designed by Ambrosia Fontaine ...
Christ–is this thing ever going to end?
SLAY

And that brings us to the end of our second annual Pageant of Darkness. Let's have a round of applause for all of our inspired creators and their muses.
clap clap clap clap clap clap clap clap cla
Finally! Can we take off now, Dave?
SLAYER

Rosa! Daaarling! You were fantastic!

C'mon ...
Hold on. I want to congratulate Rosa.
What's going on?

Um, hello? Where's that applause, people? What's going on back there?
Oh my God! Get a load of **that** idiot.
Wow. That's ... I don't know **what** that is.

Man, I **know** that guy! Who is that guy?
You **know** that guy?

Rosa, you look amazing.
That's ... it's ...

Wes.

It's Wes? Ohmigod, that **is** Wes! Hahaha-hahahahahaha!

Philistine.
Poseur.
Uncouth tourist.

When I heard, I had to ...

I brought you these.
Blood orchids! I ...

Do I know you?
... I don't believe we've met! My name's Alistair. And you are ...?

What does he think he's doing?
Let's hope he's not getting any more fashion tips.

C'mon, Jerome. Let's go congratulate Rosa.
Dave ...

... and the way the velvet just outlines ... everything. Your tailor must be **very** expensive.

And my name's Rosa, by the way.
Of course, I know. I'm Wesley.

We've met before, although I can forgive you for not recognizing me. I looked ... different, before.
Really?

Yeah, you know, Wes. From the parking lot?
Dave? The parking lot?
Yeah, last night?

The ... **surfer**?!
Yes, I'm afraid you caught me when I wasn't looking my best. And not on my best behavior, either. I apologize for my rudeness.
What?!
Oh, ha ha, don't be silly!

Oh my God, Dave, what am I going to do? He's ...
It's OK. We'll get rid of him quick ... somehow.
... absolutely perfect! He's so gorgeous I think I'm gonna **die**!

But ...

Wesley. Beautiful.
Yeah, uh, so ... nice cape.

Oh! Do you like it?! It's a traditional Transylvanian design! I got it from vampirestuff.com!
Really? I've been looking for one just like it!

Oh ... my ... God!! Where did you get those teeth! They are unbelievable! I mean, they're believable! Totally!
Ah, I can't reveal **all** my secrets!
Oh, you sassy man! Ha ha ha!

Well, the way Electronics Hut pays, I couldn't afford teeth like that in a million years, anyway. Oh, smile again, please?

That is so hot! Rrraow!
Alistair! God!

Oh, just bite my neck, please, just a little?
NO!

I mean, Wes, I need to talk to you.
Of course, David.

We'll be right back, Rosa.
And we'll be waiting!

"David"?
Nice outfit, Dave. You must have worked on that one a while.
Ha ha. And when'd you learn to put on makeup?
I was in a hair-metal band in the '80s.

Of course you were, you poseur.
We were the hottest metal band in L.A. And what crawled up your ass, anyway?

You! What the hell are you doing here?
It's called "having a good time," Dave. You should try it sometime.

Bullshit! This sn't your scene and you know it.
And it's yours? C'mon, dude. I'm just having some fun.

No, you're trying to mess with my head, you prick.
That's fun.

Are you following me around? Why do I see you so often?
What?
I'm a geek. I'm participating in a geek activity with my geek friends, checking out the cute geeky girl I like, and what the hell are you and your goddamn cheekbones doing here?

Can't a guy hang out with his little brother?

Are you out of your mind? Being murdered and made undead by the same eastern European capitalist psychopath does not make us **related**!
Well, it sorta does.
Why don't you go back to your stupid beach and leave me and Rosa alone?

Why would I want to leave Rosa alone? Have you seen her? That chick is smokin'!
That's what it **really** is, isn't it? You saw that I liked her and you're trying to mess it up.

I don't have to **try** and mess it up, ude. You'll do that just ine all by yourself. You can be her **friend** ...
Oh, screw you.

... And I'll be her "sexy friend." Simple. Good division of labor, right?
. . .

She likes me, and that drives you nuts.

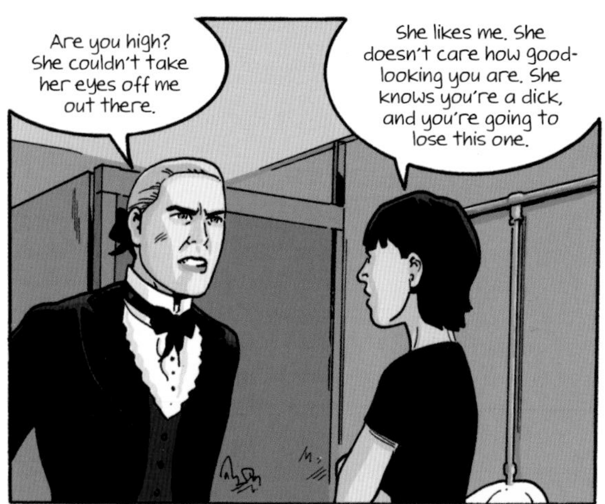
Are you high? She couldn't take her eyes off me out there.
She likes me. She doesn't care how good-looking you are. She knows you're a dick, and you're going to lose this one.

Don't be such a pinhead. Chicks are all the same. You don't even **exist** when I'm around, junior.

'Scuse me.

Do either of you have any Ultralash?

?!

Uh, no!
Nope!

This is so humiliating. You bastard!
I'm sorry my honesty upsets you, Rosa, but this is who I am.

Couldn't you have told me who you are before I wasted half a year dating you? And maybe not in the middle of **everybody**?
Frankly, I'm surprised you're being so ... conservative about this. I thought you'd be more supportive about my decision to come out.

You self-serving **cabrón**! That is **so** not the issue! Don't you try to make me the villain here.

Rosa, my passion flower.
Screw you!

My sweet, it's not like I'm totally gay. More like bisexual. We can still go out as long as you're OK with me expressing my other side ...
You want my **permission** to cheat on me?!

Wesley! Hi! We were just talking about you!
Uh, great.

Listen, babe. I gotta take off. Maybe see you around sometime?

Great. What now?

That ... **vampire** ... is going after Rosa.
Wesley, let's just go.
What are you talking about?

Whoa. That is screwed up.
No kidding. Are you going to let him get away with that?
Women are just so emotional, don't you think?
Later, dude.

What can I do about it?
Be a man! If you just lie down and let him cock-block you like that, you deserve to lose.

Thanks, buddy. *You're* a real pal.
Hold on, hold on. The situation isn't hopeless. Wes might be ridiculously good-looking and extremely rich, but you're a **really** nice guy, Dave. Rosa knows that.

That's what I'm afraid of.
Forget that crap. Dave, I'm going to give you one bit of advice and leave it at that.

Lay it on me.
Don't be such a pussy.

There she is. Go talk to her.
For God's sake do more than **talk**, Dave!

Hey.
EXIT

Huh?
Don't worry. No one's looking.

Let 'em get a good look. They're gonna live on this one for months.

DIRGE
Bitches.
You OK?

OK? What's OK?
I don't know what OK looks like.
You want me to drive you home?

You have a car?
No, uh, I mean, I could drive you in yours ... or something.

...

That's so nice of you. But I'm fine. I'll be fine.

I've got to go.
Uh ...

It was really nice of you to come.
Your dress was ... is ... really gorgeous.

You're sweet.
I mean it. It's great.

Thanks.

I'll see you later.
Uh, yeah ... you know where to find me!

Two "nices" and a "sweet."

Impressive.

Yep, I'd say she can't wait to jump your bones.
You were listening? What the hell is your **problem?**
DIRGE

Can't help it. Vampire super-hearing and all.
You have super-hearing?

You **don't**? I knew you were weak, but... man, that's **weak**.
So you're stalking me now?
Just sizing up the competition.
This isn't a contest.
DIRG

Says you. You want the girl, I want the girl. Only one of us can get the girl first. I'd say that's a contest.
I'm warning you. Leave Rosa alone.

Or what? What are you going to do about it?
...

Oooh, scary.
You know I can't fight you. I don't eat people. I don't have freaking superpowers.

Yeah, that's right!
Fine! Go ahead and hypnotize her!

That's the only way she'll ever go out with you, anyway! Vaporize into her room and super-hear her into submission! That's the real thing, Wes, yeah! Great!
I don't have to do that crap to get a girl to go out with me!

Sure, Wes, keep telling yourself that.
I'll get Rosa to go out with me without using any vampire powers. None.

You'll cheat.
You don't trust me?

Of course I don't. Why don't you just leave her alone?
"Why don't you just leave her alone?" God, Dave–Jerome's right. You're such a fucking pussy. Yeah, I heard that, too.

Fight me. Do it. Fight me for her, you pussy.
Man, I'm not fighting you!

Then she's gonna be mine! She'll be mine by my winter solstice party.
Never happen! She'll be with me! I bet you.

It's a bet, then. May the best vamp win.
And no using any powers. No hypnotism, no nothing!

No **supernatural** powers. I can't help it if I'm suave.
Swear it!

I swear.
Swear on your eyeteeth!

On my **what**?
Your fangs, you moron! It's a vampire oath, Jesus!

What did I just **do**?

Ugh, I'm so bored.
Shut up. We're surfing with Wes.
We're not surfing, we're sitting.

Stop whining! Wes isn't bored!
Shut up, George.

Don't tell me to shut up!
You're bugging Wes.

I am not, am I? Huh, Wes? Simone's annoying, right?
What?
Baby, you are really out of it. You didn't even comment on my new bikini!

Leave him alone, you bimbo. Can't you see he's thinking?
Uh, whatever! I'm the bride around here, suck up.

Shut up!
You're not even a REAL vamp. You're a bug-eating kiss ass.
Both of you, shut up.

Yeah, see?
But Wes, don't you like my bikini? I picked it out for you!
He wants to think, damn it! He's got to ... to ... are you planning something?

I don't want to talk about it.
C'mon, baby. You can tell **me**. Are you feeling down?

Simone—you an give me some advice from the emale perspective.
I sure can, baby.

So you know that chick Rosa?
That little death rocker we stalked last week?

I've been thinking about her, a lot. I can't get her to return my calls!
Well, you know what I would do is—
Goddamn it, I **knew** it! I knew you had your eye on that bitch!

Simone! Shut up.
No, George! I will **not** shut up.

... And you have Madison and Tiffani, and I stalk her for you?! You have no respect for us. This is completely insulting!

I go out and get myself a new bikini – for you! And what do you say? Nothing! Did you comment on Madison's hair yester-day? No! Do you ever–
Si-**mone**. Shut. Up.

Three vampire brides not enough for you? You have to get yourself a wetback slut on the side?

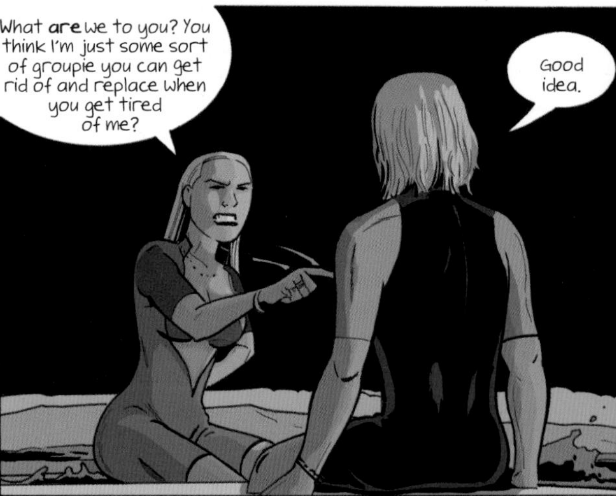
What **are** we to you? You think I'm just some sort of groupie you can get rid of and replace when you get tired of me?
Good idea.

Urk! ... Wes ... please ... no ...

Aaaaaahhhh!

Ha ha ha!

Awesome!

Surf sucks. Let's go.

Ha ha ha ...

So what's the plan? You going to creep into that Rosa's window tonight and make her an offer she can't refuse?
It's not that simple.

What's not simple? You just give her the ol' red-eye and panties'll hit the floor so fast ... man, you'll be elbows deep in pussy.
Except I can't flex the red-eye. I made this freakin' stupid bet with Dave about it.

A bet?
Well, the problem isn't the bet. I swore not to use my vampiric abilities. A blood oath.
So? Forgive me for sayin' it, but when was the last time you were worried about keeping your word?

This is different. This oath is some really ancient stuff, man. Serious vampire mojo. If I break my word and the elder vampires around town get wind of it, I'm history.
Seriously?

Yeah, man. Heavy-duty old-world tradition crap. Apparently there's some kind of lynching ritual.
Goddamn vampire immigrants.

And that little dickwad Dave tricked me into it!

He got the oath out of Radu's fricking vampire ... almanac or whatever! So he knows about the lynching ritual, and I'm in the dark! Does that sound right to you?
You never saw the book?

Oh, sure, Radu lent it to me. But what am I going to do, read it? I mean, of course Dave reads it, he's a weak-ass poindexter. But me?
All you gotta do is eat lots of people, and you're king of the world! What else do you need to know?

But of course Radu doesn't think so. Radu loves the rules. Radu loves Dave!

How can Radu prefer that weasel to me?
I'm the vampire every master wishes he made! I have vampire brides! I'll eat a guy as soon as look at him!

I'm freaking evil!

Radu is 450 years old; you'd think he'd appreciate me. But no. Dave's a "reliable employee." Dave won't even kill **criminals**. He's a spineless, powerless wuss. He's practically a **vegetarian**.

He makes me sick!

And if he thinks he's getting his clammy hands on that hot Latin ass before I do, he can just think again.

Totally. You can get any girl you want.
Hell yeah, I can. I was getting it left and right for **years** even before I was made.

What're you gonna do, bring her flowers?
Already did that.
You did? Oh, man! I was **joking**!

You want to join your friend Simone at the bottom of the ocean?
Jesus! I didn't mean anything! Take it easy!

Yeah, you're right. I need to **relax**. Maybe I'll go to Westwood and lure some drunk UCLA freshman into an alley or something.
You do that. I'm going to hang out here for a bit.

All right. See ya later.
Later.

Jesus. What a frickin' psycho.

Anyone can beeeee a brand-new looooove ...

knock knock!
What?

Phone call.
Tell whoever it is that I'm not here. I've only got half an hour until work.

Whatever you say, dude.
Rosa, I'm really sorry, but Dave's in the shower. He's been in there for hours and I have NO idea WHAT he's getting up to in there ...

Gimme that!

Hey, Rosa. What's up?

I'm booooored, Dave. Let's do something. Can you hang out?

As a matter of fact, I can. It's my night off.
No way!

AND I just got my paycheck, so whatever you want to do, it's my treat.

No way!
Shut up, dude.
MODERN Reenactor

What?

Nothing. I was just talking to my eaves-dropping roommate who needs to mind his own business. So what do you want to do?

I was hoping you had some bright ideas. I'm looking through the **Weekly** and there's noth ... ohmigod! I can't believe it!

What?
How fast can you get down to the Limelight?

The revival theater? I can be there in ... gimme half an hour.
Then I'll meet you there. Ohmi-god, this is too good to be true.

What's playing?
It's a surprise. A really, really good one. Trust me. See you there!
Bye.

I didn't know you just got paid.
I didn't.

And let me guess—you don't have the night off.
Nope.

Then ... how the heck are you going to meet Rosa at the Limelight in thirty minutes?
You're going to let me borrow your car. I've got a plan.

So let me get this straight; you want to go to the Social club ...
Yeah.

You want to convince Radu to give you the night off ...
Uh-huh.
You want me to cover your shift?
Yes.
And you want me to lend you fifty bucks?
That's the plan.

You **have** gone completely insane, haven't you? This girl better be worth it, for both our sakes.
So you'll do it?

Of course I will, you love-sick little bitch.

Thanks, man. But we've got to hurry. I'm supposed to be at work in ... jeez, fifteen minutes.
Fifteen minutes?! I won't be able to get back over there in fifteen minutes!

What about the whole mist thing?
Oh yeah. I forgot.

Can you believe all these guys hang out in a freakin' **castle**? What a cliché.
Hey, at least it's in the Hollywood Hills. They could be hanging upside down in a cave in Griffith Park.

Grooaaan ... You're really cut out to be a vampire, you know?
Oh, shut up.

No, really. Maybe they'll ask you to be their little vampire cabana boy. "Freshen up your Bloody Mary, sir? She's looking a little bit pale."
OK, OK, no more vampire jokes! Jeez!

It vas a shame!

Shame?? He vas a great actor!
Lite
Boors

Perhaps in silent film era ...
Vhy do you even care? He vas not even Romanian, he vas Hungarian!

I, too, am Hungarian.
See??!

He vas great actor! Classical! He portrayed my namesake vis such vigor!
He made za great Vlad za Impaler into a joke! A petty vampire!

Vhat iss wrong vis being vampire?
Nossing! But he vas second-rate dope fiend!

You don't talk about Bela Lugosi like that!

Oh, hello, boys.

?? Dave? Vhat are you doing here?

You should be halfvay to my store already! Shoo! Shoo!
It's just that I ... I need the night off ...

VHAT??? Night off? Dave, my childe, you put stake in my heart!
I'll cover his shift, Lord Arisztidescu! Um, I mean, if that's OK with you, my lord Vlad.

Vhat iss all zis, zis changing shifts. Vhat for?
There's this girl he likes.

Ah hah! His first vampire bride!!
Now you vill be real vampire. Blood feed! Blah ha hah!
No, it's not ... I, uh ...

Don't tell me you're not going to ... Oh, Dave. You change your mind, my childe. Of course you can have night off. Hey, I vouldn't vant to vurk you to death!! Blah hah hah!

Dave, before I do not believe. But now I see. You are ... vhat iss vurd?
Vooss.

Yes, vooss. But I have old blood at my blood bank. I cannot sell to hospital! Modern regulation be damn! So I sell to you, yes?
Ahem.

Oh, ah, yes, thank you so much, Lord Porthius.
Iss lucky night for you, Dave, no? Now quit "hanging around"!

Thank you, my lord.

Oh boy. Here we go.

the Limelight

tonight only:
THE VAMPIRUS
TRILOGY
Uncut!

the Limelight
tonight only:
THE VAMPIRUS
TRILOGY
Uncut!
Dave!
Hey there.

So what's the ...
Oh, don't worry. I already got us tickets!
THE
TRI
Uncut

Can you believe they're showing the **Vampirus** trilogy?!
Er... no?

Are you telling me you know **nothing** about the **Vampirus** films?
Not a thing. I have no idea what you're talking about.

They're only, like, the rarest vampire movies ever!
Oh yeah?

They were made in Italy in the late '60s by Abermarle Hotchkiss, a drugged-out, British, mad-genius-director guy. I saw another film he did, **Blood Coven of Soho**, and it was fantastic. **Totally** psychedelic.

You're some kind of film geek, aren't you? I mean, you know, that's rad, but I need to know.
Ha ha ha ha ha!

You want popcorn?
I'm a **selective** film geek. These films are always being talked about in the goth 'zines. They're legendary. Apparently, Hotchkiss took the money the studio gave him to make a sequel to **Blood Coven** ...
... and instead he made, like, a six-hour movie about this wandering vampire beatnik named Vampirus.
The studio cut it up into three separate films, released them, and forgot them. Hotchkiss went crazy—he shot himself with a harpoon gun in '72 on a party boat in Mallorca.

A harpoon?
And all the prints of the movies vanished.

Wow. Intense.

And thanks to the efforts of my dad, pretty soon you will be able to replay the **Vampirus** movies over and over to your dark heart's content on DVD special editions.
Wes?!

I grew up watching these movies. They're, like, my childhood favorites.
Qué mentiroso. Nobody's seen the **Vampirus** movies for thirty years.

Nobody but me and my buddies. These are my dad's prints they're screening tonight.
Your dad's?

Yeah. He's a movie producer. He bought the whole catalog of this Italian movie company back in the late '70s when they went bankrupt. Me and my buds used to get stoned and have marathons of all this shit in our family screening room.

It was your fashion show that convinced me there was a market for this stuff.
Really?

Totally. I convinced my dad to license all of the **Vampirus** films out to a cult DVD company. This screening is sort of a promotional thing.
Yeah, right.

C'mon, Dave! You of all people should know how much I love cool vampire stuff.

You never told me Wes liked this sort of stuff.
I never knew.

I've got to get to the front; I'm supposed to introduce this thing.
Oh, OK, see you later!

Yeah, so, uh, return one of my phone calls one of these days, OK?

Excuse me a minute, Rosa.

What the hell are you doing here? Are you following us? You swore: no powers.
Take it easy, Dave. This is really and truly a total coincidence, I swear. My dad totally owns these movies.

And you've been calling Rosa?
Hey, man: vampires use telephones, too.

Dave?

Stay away from us.
Don't worry, buddy. I'll sit a couple of rows back so you can feel her up in peace.

Screw you, dickhead.
Oh, and Dave?

What?
These movies really are pretty awesome.

Three Psychotronic Vampire Movies Later ...
the Limelight
tonight only:
THE VAMPIRU
TRILOGY
Krrrr—rrr-rrr...

Is it totally dead?
Yep. Do you have a cell phone? I need to call my tío Joaqui and get him to come give me a jump.

Isn't it a bit late?
Yeah, but I gotta get home.

I'll give you a ride.
You don't mind driving all the way to Boyle Heights?

No, not at all. It's Carl's car, anyway.
That's great, thanks. I'll call my uncle in the morning.

I just hope your car'll be OK.
Who's going to mess with that beater?

Good point.
Guy, Dave. You weren't supposed to agree with me.

So what'd you think about the movies? Weren't they great?

Yeah, I guess. It's just...
I know it's hardly a documentary, but doesn't that whole tortured-vampire-prince thing seem a little ... far-fetched to you?

What do you mean?
Don't you think a vampire, a real vampire, would have too much practical stuff to worry about to mope around Europe on a motorcycle?

"Practical" stuff? He's an immortal!
Sure, but how would he make rent on his lair? That place was pretty swank, too.

He has to lay out cash to make sure the locks are secure where he sleeps. Not to mention getting good enough sun coverage on the windows. That stuff costs money, you know.

Gee, Dave. You've put a lot of thought into this. Ever heard of artistic license? Suspension of disbelief?
Well, I'll say this for it: The music rocked. Somebody needs to release that stuff. Acid rock with a choir **and** an orchestra? Bitchin'.

Take a left here.
Maybe Wes should ask his dad to do it. Do you think he was telling the truth about that?
STOP

Wes is a spoiled Malibu rich kid, so I suppose the idea of his dad being some oily film producer isn't outrageous.
I think that's pretty ... interesting, don't you?

Turn right.
Eh. I bet his dad is in jail for stock fraud.

Ha ha ha ha ha.

Do you think he really called, or is he just screwing with me?
I wouldn't know.

Goddamn it. My mom is always doing this!
Doing what?

Trying to run my life. Sabotaging me. She drove Alistair away. Which is not to say I'm sorry he's gone.
I thought Alistair was gay?

Ptch. No. He just es to play at it. He's ready sleeping with ianita. Turn left at the corner.
But what does that have to do with ...?

My parents think I should be married already. Or close. To a Mexican guy. I should be getting a full-time job, getting pregnant ...
Really?
They don't get what I'm trying to do! I want to be a designer! They think I'm not a good daughter.
I stopped going to church last year, and that was pretty much it for my dad. He barely speaks to me these days.

It's in the middle of the next block.
I'm sure they'll understand once you make it big ...

Heh. Sure.

Here we are. Oh, and look, lights on, waiting up for their delinquent daughter. You'd think Ma would be in bed. She has to be at work in about six hours.
Wow, that's harsh.

Does she want me to have to work in a sweatshop all my life, too?
Well, she's an Amor de los Amores fan, so she can't be all that bad.

I gotta go. Thank you for tonight. I had a great time.
Me too. Talk to you tomorrow?

Sure.

<Who was that?>
<None of your business, but it's my friend Dave.>

<You and your white boys. Why won't you go out with Rogelio? And what happened to your car?>
<Ma, do I have any messages?>

<Another white boy.>
<You can't keep me from seeing whoever I want!>

<You'll understand how I worry when you have children of your own, God willing.>

This is Wes, and I'm not answering the phone for a very, very good reason. Leave a message. Or don't. Whatever.

Dario Argento and Cary Grant. What a power twosome.
You and your Cary Grant.
please rewind

"Are **you** referring to **me,** Madam?!"
Yep, you're a true creature of the night, make no mistake.

Hey, man, my life is enough of a horror show as it is. Give me screwball any day!
You could take a lesson from this ...

Whoa!
Hey!

Oh, hey, Rosa, what's up?
Oh my God, Dave, you almost gave me a heart attack!
Hey, Rosa.

You just getting off work?
Yeah. You watching some movies?
Yeah: **His Girl Friday** and **Suspiria**.
Wow, that's some double feature.

I'm gonna get the car.
I know, that's what I said. But you know Carl and his cheesy horror flicks. You want to join us?

Um, yeah, that would be great, but, uh ...
Well, you know, that's cool ... I just ...

But I have a date ...

Yeah, so, it's actually really funny ...
... that's great ...

I mean, you won't believe it, it's sort of embarrassing, but, so, after we ran into him, I started talking to him on the phone a bit, and, um, since then, we've gone out a couple of times ...
Wait ...

Who are you going out with?
Um, with Wes.

But but but! It's not like you think! He's really sweet and gentlemanly.
Sweet?! He's a monster! He's just playing with you! I can't believe you'd be so gullible!

Because you know him so **well**, right?
I know him better than you could ever...

Screw you, Dave! He's been nicer to me than any other guy ever has!
Then you've obviously had too many shitty boyfriends to know the difference.

Oh, but you know what's good for me?
I'm serious, Rosa – stay away from Wes.

So, now you're forbidding me to see him? Just beautiful.

Rosa! Wait!
Go to hell!

Wow, what was that all about?

Yeah, sure. No, it's no problem.
But what kind do you want?

Uh, we have Captain Sugar, Whizzies, Health Flake, and Choco Snackies.

You want Health Flake??

Captain Sugar. That's more the Carl I know and love.

Oh, I'm fine.
I'm thinking about giving away the register and abandoning the store so Radu will find me and kill me.

Ding-a-Ling!
Oh, man – you won't believe who's walking through the door.
Bingo. Gotta go.

Dave! My man!

Wes. What do you want? Need to buy eighteen cases of Blood Brew?
Naw, dude, I was just in the area, thought I'd stop by to see if Radu was around. See what's up with the old Transylvanian Social Club.

No, you didn't. Give me a break. You're just trying to bust my balls.
Don't you think they ought to let me into that club?

Yeah, whatever.
It's totally racist not to let American vampires in, don't you think?

What are you **talking** about? You seriously want to "hang" with me? After you've been sneaking around with Rosa behind my ...
Whoa! She didn't tell you? Hey, I thought you guys were **best friends** ...!

Very funny, dickweed.
How was I supposed to know? I thought **girlfriends** told each other **everything**!

I'm going to kill you!
Bring it on, shorty. Hey, while I'm here, get me a case of Blood Brew, will ya?

Hell no! Get the hell out of here!
Hey hey hey ... why must we fight, my brother? We can't let some Bauhaus bitch get between us.

Don't talk about her that way.
Come on, just admit that you've lost our little bet, and let it go. Bros before ho's, after all.
Ding-a-ling!

Get. Out.
Oh, you wanna piece? OK, let's go!
I'm not gonna fight you.

Ha ha. That's why you'll never get the girl. No balls.
Ugh, God, why can't you just **leave**?
Man, we can't let some piece of tail come between us! You're the closest thing to a brother I have!

Only since you **murdered** your actual brother.
Don't talk about things you don't understand.

You're a certifiable sociopath. You delight in ruining the lives of others ...
Whatever.

Mine, Rosa's, your poor brother's ...
Shut up!

No wonder Radu got rid of you. Not even he could stand ...
Shut **UP**!
Ugh! Watch it!
... bunch of **thugs**! Disgusting!

Get lost, you mascara-wearing freaks!
Surfer! Oh my God, gross! Look at that Neanderthal! He looks like he's been cooked on a spit!

Just go, Wes. I'm sick of looking at you.
No one tells me what to do!
Look at those two macho idiots. They're just like the jocks at school! Always fighting!

I've got no use for you, Radu doesn't want you around ...
Aaagh!
Eeek! Aaah!

Oh my God, the window! Radu's gonna ...

AAAAH! Vhat has happen to my store! Vhat iss going on here? Vhy iss my vindow in pieces on za ground?
It's not my fault! Wes ...

Vess?! Dave!
... uh ...

... and so Radu blew his stack, and said the whole thing was my fault, because I should be out killing people and drinking their blood.
What? Why? That's crazy!
The Sunshine Diner

No, well, he thinks I'm pathetic. He's totally old-world. He's never heard of a vegetarian.
It's still not your fault.

He thinks that if I had "powers" I could have stopped Wes, or at least protected the window.
I still don't get how he knew it had happened so fast.
He has like a deep spiritual connection to his money.

So he cut off your blood bank supply.
Yeah, no more past-dated blood for me. He thinks I'll get desperate and go hunt, but it's not going to happen. So I guess I'll just wither away and die.
Awww. Poor baby.

I'm serious. I don't see any other way! I have no idea where I'll get anything to eat, and, anyway, I'm sort of an abomination in the eyes of God, so whatever. You know, maybe it's time. Ugh, so hungry!
grblgrblgrbl

e'll think of something. omato juice doesn't work, does ? Anyway, you can't leave Rosa to Wes.
That's the worst part. I hope I can do something about it before I waste away completely.

At least Wes can't hang at the Last Stop anymore.

So, Dave, vee understand each osser. I only try to make you real "man."

Yes, Master.

And you! Vess! You vill not enter my store again! I fire you to keep you **away** from my store. Look how much money you lose me. Again!

But, Lord A!

Vhat deed you call me?

Um, Lord Arisztidescu! How am I going to be able to spend money here?

Ah, yes. Hum, yes, zis iss problem.

Yes, you VILL shop here. But you vill phone order to Dave and vait outside! Now begone! And vindow goes on your bill!

But ...

BE GONE.

Don't be such a loser, Dave. You have all eternity to get with this girl, and you've only hung out with her for, what, a few weeks? You just have to say something to her about how you feel.
Sue-Yun's right. The girl's not psychic.

She's dating Wes. Do I look like I can compete in that department?
No.

You guys are on to something.
Dave will never beat Wes at his own game.
Thanks a LOT, Jerome.
It does seem unlikely.

You guys are pathetic! You think all a girl wants is a big slab of beef?
Well ...

Forget it. You're hopeless. I've got to get my uniform on.
No, c'mon, Sue-Yun, I want your point of view. You're a girl, right?

Thank you, Dave. I may be dead, but it's still nice to be noticed. You want my advice? Take the lady to the beach or something, have a long walk, tell her funny stories and how gorgeous she looks and stuff, and then tell her you're really into her, so, no pressure, but would she like to go on a date?

That is, like, the scariest thing I have ever heard in my life!
Oh **come on!**

Nope. Can't do it. She'll have to develop her psychic abilities.

Suit yourself. I'm right. My shift's about to start ...

I really dig you, Sue-Yun. No pressure, but do you want to go on a date?
Ha ha ha! In your dreams, bwah!
Aaagh! See?!?!

Mm-mm-mmm. That is one fine vampire waitress. When I go Blacula, she is all mine!
You're gonna have to suck a lotta hot plasma to tame that tiger.

You have to call her, though. You just can't leave her to Wes.
I know. I know! I know.
You loser.

Let me use your phone.

I'm sorry but ... I just don't understand what you **see** in him. He's such a ... such a ... surfer **idiot**.
But you know, the thing is, I think that whole "jock" thing is just a pose, you know?
Oh?

Yeah, seriously. You wouldn't believe what a softie he is when he's alone!
You're right: I wouldn't.

I mean, he's just like, **so nice**, you'd never expect it. So attentive. And I think his tan is fading. You won't believe what he said to me!
What?

He was like, "Rosa, you aren't like anyone I've ever met. You're such a free person. I wish I were more like you."
That's ... great.

Yeah, I mean, he's free, too, but he just doesn't see it, you know? He keeps himself all bottled up.
Yeah, I'm sure.

Dave, I am **so glad** you called me. You are such a **great friend**. I didn't want to lose you over this.
You won't lose me. I'll always be your ... friend.

I'm sorry if I'm being boring! He's just **so romantic**, and after Alistair ... I feel like a big goon! I'm not usually like this! I'm so glad I can talk to you. No one else understands.
I ...

Uh-
oh.

Wes?
Oh, hey, Rosa. What are you doing here?

What's up with **you**?
Who are those girls?

This is Tiffani, and this is Madison. T&M, this is Rosa.
Heyyyy.

But who **are** they?
That's just none of your business.

None of my ... are we not going out?
Sure we are. But I'm a free man. You said it yourself.

Not **that** free! Get rid of them!
Not a chance, babe.

I refuse to be in the same room with those bimbos!
Suit yourself. But we're not leaving.

So, are you going? You're blocking the waitress.

Later, Sue-Yun. Put some poison in his blood, willya?
With pleasure.

C'mon, let's go. Let's take a walk.

But why did he have to walk into **that** diner?
Er ... It's a hangout, you know ... but isn't it better that you know?

No. Yes. I suppose.

... I'm just so sorry I yelled at you the other day. You were right, I was wrong.
No, Rosa ...

God! I'm so **stupid**! All he wanted was a piece of ass!
You **slept** with him?!

No, it's ... It's just ... Oh, Dave!

I should have known
he wasn't really into me.
He's got **everything**.
Everything I **don't** have.
He's blond and tan and ...
You don't even **like** tans.

The point being: he's **white**. And he's rich. He's just ...
And that makes him superior?

No, of course it doesn't. But then, in the eyes of the world, of course it does. A guy like that? With a little Mexican wetback chick? Never happen.
You know what they call Goths in Mexico? Darks. Makes ya think.

And the list just goes on: he's a WASP. He's unbelievably hot.
Ungh.
He's even **tall**.

It's just so totally unfair. He has **everything**, just by virtue of being born.

Everything, and then he's a total asshole. Selfish, selfish white boy.
I don't **want** to want him. I just can't help myself.

The only way I'll ever get any respect is if I win the goddamn lottery.
Rosa, no ...

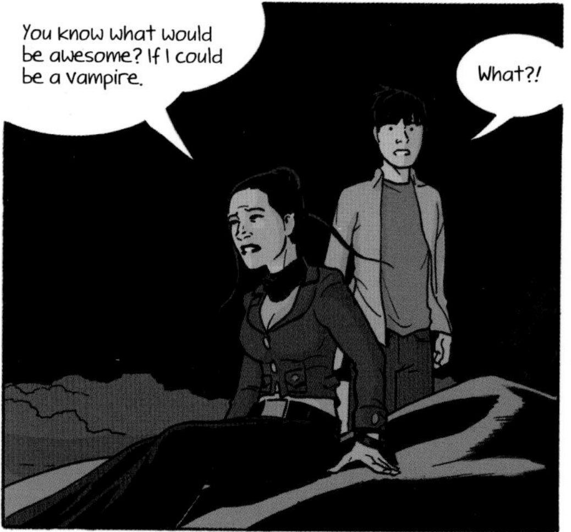
You know what would be awesome? If I could be a vampire.
What?!

I'm serious. That would fix everything.
But **why**? You mean like Alistair?

Uch. That idiot. No. Of course not. I mean a **real** one. Like Vampirus.
Rosa, come on.

No, I mean it. Don't you think it's possible they're out there, really? There wouldn't be so much lore if they didn't exist.
OK, fine. Let's just say there **are** vampires, and you coul become one ... how would that help?

It would be power, Dave. Clearly. And money, and community.
You have community. What about your family?

You can keep it.
But do you really know anything about them? Vampires?

I've read all the lore. I know it inside out.
But what if it's not true? What if it's just made up by humans?

Anne Rice is a human, as far as we know, right? How would she know?
What if they're not all rich? What if they have regular crappy jobs?

What are you talking about?
Well look. Are they rich from the minute they're made? Where do they get their money?

The community takes care of its own ...
But what if it doesn't? What if it's just pure capitalism? They'd have to make young vampires just to work for them, like slaves!

I don't ...
But then, they have to live on blood, right? That's a limited resource. How many people can they get away with killing before they start drawing the attention of law enforcement?

They can live on animal blood.
You don't know that. What if they can't? What if it's only human blood that works? Then what?

grblgrblgrbl
Ooops!

Are you hungry?
Yeah, but, I'm, um, fasting. To cleanse my system.

But so, anyway, you have these vampires, fighting for a limited food source. They make new vampires to make money for them. And what about those young vampires?
Probably most of them are just like me, working schlubs. No way up, no way out. You know? Not pretty.

And you're a vegetarian!
That's different.

Blood: not vegetarian.
I'd manage!

You ready to murder people?
Dave, don't be a jerk!

It's just that I think you're ignoring some essential parts of the equation. The blood, the murder. The money. And, you know, eternity is a really long time. What if you were stuck with a bad master?
You're so literal. I think it would be cool.

I picture this vast network of dark, beautiful, intellectual, and artistic people, living forever with only the best things, the best food, the best clothes, beautiful homes ...

They take themselves away from all the horrendous fashion and the filthy strip malls, the half-dead palm trees, and the smog and the racism and the snobbery ...

st Stop
Ta

It would just be a better life, living amidst beauty and with all the time and energy in the world to concentrate on the finer things. I hate LA.

acho
city

I only wish you could be right.
I know.

Now I just need to meet some!
Rosa, I'm absolutely **sure** you will meet some. But maybe you won't know it.

I think I would sense it. Maybe there's one here, tonight!
You think so?

Don't worry, Dave, he won't bite us. Anyway, I don't really think so. I don't feel it. Why would a vampire go to the beach, anyway?
Because it's beautiful?

Yeah, the moon really is nice tonight.

Honey, I'm home!
Oh, darling! I missed you! How was work?

Made lots of money on the stock market today. Looks like that trip to Europe will be coming sooner than we thought!
Dave ... my lord ... Do you sink you could find it in your heart to take an old vampire vis you on a trip back to za Muzzerland?
Aw, get stuffed with garlic, you old bat! You've got sweeping to do!
Dave, you were so kind to keep Radu on as your servant after you took over his empire and broke his spirit.
I guess I was, wasn't I?
Oh, Dave!
Dave?
Dave? Dave? Where are you, Dave?
I'm right here.

Ahhh, you smell amazing. Would you smell so good if you were a vampire?
Yes, my master.

Rosa? Are you OK?
Yes, my master.

Oh my God, I've hypnotized her! I didn't even know I knew how to do that!

I could just take a sip, just a taste, and she'd never know. I could make it look like she scratched herself. She wouldn't ever ...

But that'd be cheating! Wes would find out.

But I wouldn't be doing it to get her to love me, just to eat something! And to have it be her ...

What am I doing? I must be crazy! I have got to get out of here before I do something very, very wrong!

Rosa. You will wake up in two minutes, return to your car, and drive home.
You will remember that you dropped me off at the diner so I could pick up my bike.

You will hug your mom and remember that she loves you, even if she's a little annoying sometimes.
Yes, my master.

AAAAH!

crap!

Ahh! Damn it! Man! Damn, that smarts!

Man, you haven't had **anything**, have you? Look at you, you're hardly bleeding!

Oh, man! But my backpack is!
I can't afford to lose any!

Hey, you two! Stop!
Remind me again why this is better than getting it fresh?

Don't start, man! This is bad enough as it is. You don't think I feel like a total loser for stealing blood from a blood bank?
Even if it's Porthius's blood bank?

Hey, don't bogart.

Yum. Stale.

My life sucks, and I never die.

There you are, you freaks!

Whoa!

Man, you look bad.

Here, you need this more than I do.

What am I going to do?
I don't want to be the one to suggest it, but ...

Out of the question.
But you're in bad shape, dude. What are you going to do?

I wish I had it in me to just fast until I wither away, or run out in the sun and end it.

But I'm weak. I hypnotized Rosa. By accident. I almost bit her. If I'm not careful, I'm going to be out killing people without even knowing I'm doing it.
Survival instinct.

I guess this is one way to get your daily nutrition.

If "Guinness is good for you," 100 percent fermented blood must be better.

Christ, Dave. Slow down.

!

!

What happened to you?!
Chase ... chase-ed by dogs. Biiiig ...

Dogs.

Dave? Are you OK?
He's drunk, is what he is.
Wha?

Dave, Rosa came by a little while ago.
Rosa? Heyyyy ...
What happened?

Uh, I'hm OK ... no worries. OK. Just a lil' scratch.

Let me see!
No no no! OK! I'm OK! Why're you here? What ...?

Tsst! Ooh, that looks bad. Carl, get a rag, OK?
Rosa, I'm so happy to see you. I missed you SO MUCH.

...

I juss wiss tings was worked out better.
Things ...

So beautiful. So beautiful.

Juss wanna be 'round you.

... love you ...

Right back atcha, mi amor.

Rosa!
Hi. I thought I'd come visit you before you go to work.

I'm not dressed ... ha ha ha ...

... how did you get in?
Carl. He's watching TV. You should get up soon. Your show's almost on.

It smells like boy in here.
Yeah, well.

You should ...
No!

... open the window.

What, are you allergic to hygiene?
Siiigh ... ha ha, you're right.

I'm always right.

Wow. You **are** right.
Ha ha ha!

Dave? Hey, Dave? I don't want to intrude, but ...
knock knock

Wha? What is it?
It's just that, it's like, almost nine. You're going to miss work if you're not careful.

Nine?!
Nine?!! **¡Maldición!** I'm late for work!! **¡Puta madre!** Carl! Why didn't you wake me up?!
What do I look like? Dave's butler?

Agh!

I'll call you!

Whatta woman.
Man, you better treat that one right! Danger, Will Robinson!

Hey, can I get some help here?
5.49
4.99
Ding-a-ling!

Why, of course, sir!
This here milk expires tomorrow!
STAFF ON

Oh no! Let me get you another carton!

Let's see—December 15, December 21 ... Here you are. I'm so sorry, I hadn't rotated the milk yet this evening. My apologies.
Oh, that's OK.

That'll be $2.95.
You have a good night, now.

And you, too! Have a great week, in fact!

Dave, you are picture of good employee! I know I do right sing to take you off plasma.

Yep! cheers! Ha ha!

You are drunk?! Zis iss vhy you make nice vis customer?
Ding-a-ling!

How else could I survive? Don't worry. I paid for it.
That iss not issue, you must **hunt** ...
Rah-dooo! My man!

How is my best Socal distributor?
Piotr. You are here.

Pete, Radu. Left Piotr in the old world, along with my cape. This is America, buddy. Get with the program.
Shameful, to **sell** blood beer. It iss za end of za traditions ...

Heyyyyyy, check it out: You let your employees partake of my product while on the job! Excellent!
In my day, vee all brew. Good, **strong** home brew. Not zis veak ...

Sales up 15 percent in the last two months. Nice work, Rad.
15 percent??

Just keep this up, and you'll be my top national distributor ...
Dave?!

I'm rolling out some **great** new products soon; your customers will **love** them. Blood Pale Ale, Blood Weiss ...
I get plasma from Porthius tonight. I put in fridge in back.

So, I'll put you down for three cases each?
Iss master's job to make childe strong, Dave. I vill not stop to try.

Howdy, beautiful!

What are **you** doing here?
Hey hey, now. I just wanted to drop off this invitation–I'm having a party on Saturday, my annual winter solstice party.

Oh, great. Should I wear my bikini? Dye my hair blonde for you?
You know I'm going out with Dave.
Oh yeah, sure. This invite is for you **and** the Davester.

See? You know, I'm happy for you. And lil' Davey.
Dave.

Dave. Right. Where is he, anyway? I haven't seen him around in forever.
He's at work. As usual.

Yeah, a little odd, that one. I can never figure out what he's up to ...
We might make it, I dunno.

Oh! I almost forgot.

I brought you something. To watch on those long days when Dave's not around.
What?

A preview copy of the **Vampirus** box set.
No way! That's amazing!

Heh, well. I know you've probably got a lot of hours to fill.

What the hell is that supposed to mean? If you've got something to say, Wes, just say it.
I was just joking! I just think Dave's a bit strange, that's all. He's so pale and squirrelly.

Yeah, so? I'm pale, too.
Not as pale as he is, chiquita. I don't think that boy ever sees the light of day.

He works at night!
I know, I know! But isn't it more than that? I don't think I've ever seen the boy even eat ... Well, you know him better than I do. It all probably makes perfect sense to you.

It does!
OK, well, anyway, hope to see you guys at the party!

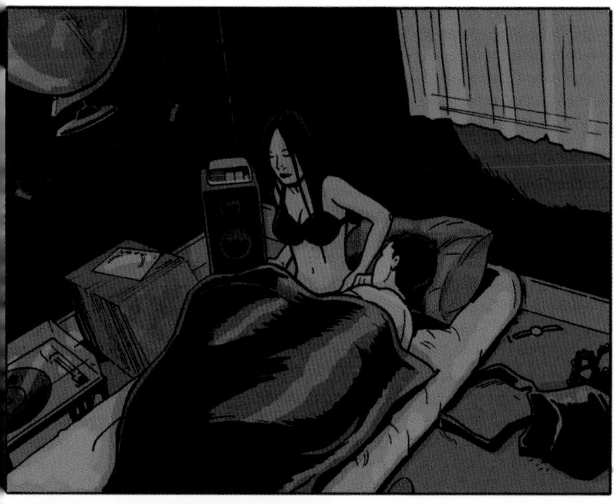

12:00 PM

Dave? Amor, it's noon. I have to go in half an hour.

Mph. Hi.
Hi. You want some coffee?

No, I'm fine. I'll have some V8 in awhile.
I don't know how you can drink that stuff first thing in the morning.

So, how was work yesterday?
It was OK. Slow. Janice was pissed that I was late, but she'll get over it.

Wes came in to see me.
Oh?

He brought me the **Vampirus** box set.
That was awfully thoughtful of him.

I don't know why you can't believe he can be nice sometimes.
I know him a lot better than you do.

Not according to him.
What?

He invited us to a party—for the winter solstice.
Oh, great.

I think we should go. He's trying to be friends.
Don't be so ...

Don't say "naive." Don't you dare.
OK, whatever.

Let's go out for breakfast. Brunch. We never do that.

You don't have time. You have to get to class.
I could skip.

And I need to get some more sleep!

Dave?
What?

Is there anything you want to tell me?

No.

Yes there is! Don't lie to me!
What did Wes say to you?

Are you cheating on me?
What?!

Are you **cheating** on me?
No! Is that what he said? Jesus.

He didn't say that. I said that.
What possible reason ...

What do you do all day?
I sleep! I work at night!

All day? How much sleep does a person need?
I play a video game. I eat dinner. What do you want from me?

We have **never** gone out to dinner. Do you go eat behind my back?
No! You know I can't afford restaurants!

Let's have a picnic! Let's go to the park!
Why am I suddenly under attack? Is it my fault I'm poor?

The park is free!

So we'll go to the park tonight.

Not tonight. Now.
Rosa, I can't ...

Why, you have to sleep? I'm supposed to believe that?
No, um ...

I'm **so sick** of this crap!
No!

LYWOOD

The lying, the deception ...

Dave?
OLLYW

What the hell is your problem?
I'm ... very allergic to the sun. I get hives.

Oh, right. Sure. Are you allergic to food, too?
Uh ...

What are you not telling me? What is it? Are you on drugs?
No, no ...

Carl?
Hey, it's none of my business ...

What's not your business?
Don't listen to him.
Dave. Just tell her. You have to tell her sooner or later.

Shut up!
Tell me what?
Dude, it's eventually gonna come out ...

Shut up!
What?!
Rosa, this is gonna sound kinda weird, I know ...

Carl, NO!
I mean, he's really a good guy, but ... he's a vampire.

Crap! Ow ow!
I'm, uh, I'm going out.

Ow ow ow ...

Slam
You ...

Rosa, I ...
It's not true. You're making fun of me.

I wish I were.
It's true.

So, vampires really exist, and you're **one of them**, and you didn't even tell me?
How can you imagine that would be OK?

The one thing I tell you I truly want ...
You were fantasizing!

If you love me, you'll make me a vampire. Right here, right now.
No! I won't do it **because** I love you.

Look at me! I work like a slave for my master! I'm broke! I can't even go out in the sun! Is that romantic? Does it sound **fun**? I'm supposed to be out **killing** people!
You kill people?

No! But I'm **supposed** to!
See? See? You don't have to be a murderer! You lied to me, you've been lying all along!

Does Wes know? Does everyone know?
Ptch. "Does **Wes** know?" **I'd** say so.

Rosa, where are you going?

Rosa. Please. I don't want to ruin your life ...

Oh, don't worry. You won't.

Rosa!

Rosa! Don't leave! I'll tell you everything!

I'll tell you anything you want to hear!

Uh ... sorry?

Dave, listen, just give her a couple of days to cool down, then call her up and apologize. Get down on your knees if you have to.
I don't think that'll work.
Neither do I.

What are you talking about? That ALWAYS works with chicks! The first couple of times, at least.
Not this time. She, uh ... she found out about Dave's little secret.

What secret? Oh ...
"Found out"?!
I **said** I was sorry! She was gonna find out eventually!

So she freaked out?
Are you kidding? She wants to **be** one of us!
You have to admit, she took the whole "learning vampires are real" thing really, really well.

And you said no? You could've had your own vampire love slave! What a loser!

I want to die.
Heartbreak's a bitch. The only thing for it ...

Is to get right back on the horse.
Forget it. I'm not letting you set me up.
Who said anything about that? Wes's party is tonight. We're going.

You want me to cheer up by hanging out with Wes? Now I **know** you've lost your mind.
I know you hate the guy, Dave, but facts are facts: He throws a wicked party.
Don't be stubborn, man. Let's go! I wanna see this.

You what?
It's a party at this crazy-rich vampire's beach house. That's ... interesting.
And there'll be hot babes.

And there'll be hot babes.
Whatever.
And lots of Blood Brew!

Wow. Look at this place.

Yeah, sure, but your place is way better. It's ... real.
A real dump, you mean. No wonder Wes hated working at the Last Stop.
Jeez, Carl. Loosen your lips from the guy's butt already.

I'm not ... I wasn't ... Damn, man. I was just digging the house.
Yeah, Dave. Lighten up a little.
Forget it. I'm gonna go find myself a beer.

You know, you could try giving us a break here. We're only trying to help.
By taking me to my archenemy's party. Gee, thanks.

"My archenemy"? Jeez! Listen to you, Mr. Delusions of Grandeur. C'mon ...

Cut it out! I'm not in the mood, Jerome.
Well, fine then. Sit here and brood. I'm gonna go see if I can't get up to some trouble. Later, grumpy.

This seat taken?
Wha ...?

Oh, hey, Merle. Good to see you.
Likewise.

What are you doing here, anyway? You **hate** Wes.
Free brew, son. Wouldn't miss drinking on Pretty Boy's bill.
I hear ya.

I could ask you the same question. You ain't too fond of our host either.
Jerome and Carl dragged me here. They thought it would cheer me up.

What's the matter?
You know that girl I was dating, Rosa?

Yeah?
We broke up.

What, just now?
No, yesterday. Why?

Well, shit. Hate to be the guy to give you the heads-up, but she's here.
She's at the party?!

Yeah, man. I saw her talking to Wes and figured she came with you.
She was talking to Wes? When? Where?

About a half hour ago, upstairs. Hey, uh ...?

Rosa!

Hey!

Hey, Dave.
What's up?
Merle says
Rosa's here.
Have you seen
her?

No, I ...
Rosa!
Are you up
here?

Aaaaah!
Rosa! Nooo!

You bastard!
Let her go!
Too late
for you, my
friend.

Rosa!

Dave?
You ...

You **made** her?! I'm going to kill you!
Ah ah ah! She wanted it, Davester.

You broke your oath! The council will have your neck.
Wait a minute there, bro. I'm telling you, little miss wannabe came straight to me and **begged** me to turn her into a vampire. Ask her.

Is that true?
Don't be like that! ***You*** wouldn't do it!

I was trying to protect you!
When are you going to learn that I don't need protection?! I don't want it!

But how did you know? About him?
I may not have figured **you** out, but I'm not an idiot. You practically told me yourself.

And he just ... did it to you?
Yep. No hypnotism, no powers, no nothing. She just ... asked me. So it looks like I win after all, huh? Damn, that was easy!

Oh, Rosa, I can barely look at you ...
Querido, I'm so sorry. I didn't mean ...

I feel so strange. Not like I thought I would. Can we just go home? Please?

Sure. I'm too tired to argue. Let's get out of here.
You're staying.

No.

I say, yes.
Dave? I can't move! What's happening?!

He can't help you now. I made you, that means you're mine. Sorry, sweetie. Them's the rules.

No, it's true, I've always had a deep interest in yoga ...

What the ...?

I'll KILL you!
You and what army, little bro?

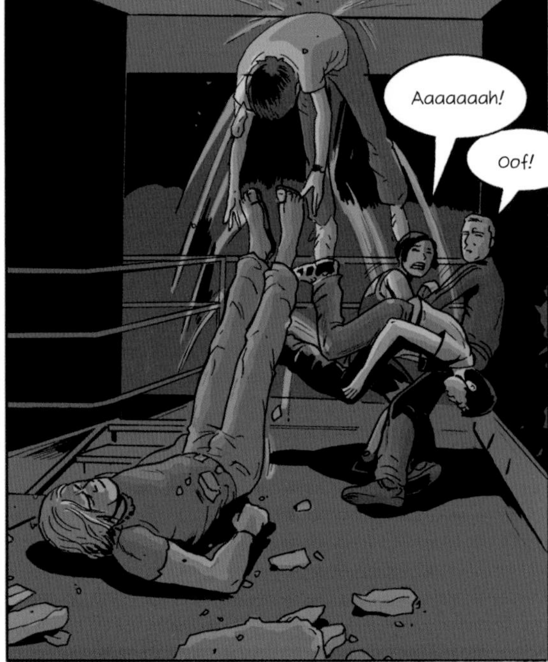
Aaaaaaah!
Oof!

Dave, what's going on?
You guys were just saying your goodbyes, weren't you?

I don't think so.
Dave! Don't!

Aah! Get off me!

Have you lost your mind, Dave? You don't drink real blood, man! You have no chance against me.

That's it.
No!

Dave!
Oh shit, oh shit, oh shit, oh shit.

Uhhh ... oh, God.

You had enough?
Go to hell. You raped my girlfriend.

I didn't do anything she didn't want me to. But that sort of accusation really hurts my feelings, and for that, I'm going to have to really take it out of you.

I wanna see if I can get you all the way into the ocean with this one ...

OW!
Let him go.

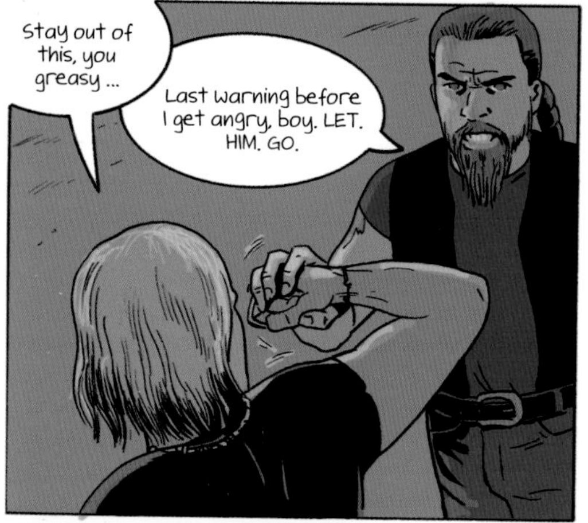
Stay out of this, you greasy ...
Last warning before I get angry, boy. LET. HIM. GO.

Crunch! Snap!
Aaaah! OK, OK!

All of you, get off my property. Now!

We were just leaving.

Except for you, Rosa. You'll stay, won't you?

I can't go with you, Dave. I can't!
I know.

I didn't hear you. Won't you be staying?
Yes, Master.

That's more like it.

Jesus. What a crappy party.

So how'd you talk Wes into letting you move out?
Seriously? I have no idea.

Sue-Yun, I was so scared. Last week he went crazy—he murdered Tiffani and Madison right in front of me. He ripped their heads off. I just...

I thought I was next. He was so angry. But, instead, he just kept walking around me, mumbling something in Latin. Turns out it was an "emancipation ritual."
Really? I didn't know there was such a thing. Wow. I'm so jealous.

I didn't either. I still don't know why he did it. But ... it's so much better.

But now I need a job.
But you don't have to work here. You could do anything!

I know, but I need a job right away. I have to get some money together to get my own place. As it is, it's getting hard to explain to my mom why I'm sleeping all day.
Welcome to the life. So to speak.

Thank you.
We vampire sisters have to stick together.

Dave, mark zis down, I take one box blood jerky, and one six-pack Blood Brew. Iss horrible stuff, but Porthius loves it. Vhat can I do?
Radu?

Yes?

I just wanted to say ... thank you for what you did for Rosa. I really appreciate it.
Vas no problem. Anysing for good employee. Iss ironic, no? Only because I am master of Vess, I can force heem to renounce Rosa, and be master to no one.

So Rosa's really free?
Yes. Free forever. But I am not sinking zis best idea, Dave. New vampire needs firm guiding hand of master. Like me to you.

Let's hope Rosa makes it despite that terrible handicap.
Yes, vell, iss her business now. But not to forget: vee make bargain, you and me.

Believe me, I haven't forgotten.
Aren't you late for your card game?
You are right! I go.

Ding-a-ling!
HELP WANTED

Last Stop

Ding-a-ling!

Excuse me, are you the manager?
Why do you ask?

Uh ... Help Wanted?
Ah.

You're OK with working nights?
Sure. You quitting or something?

No, as a matter of fact, I'm opening up a new location over on Pico.
I'll work anytime. I really need this job, man. I'm almost out of the money I moved here with.

Oh yeah? Where you from?
Ohio. I'm trying to start a band.

Oh, really ... Ohio, huh? Your family miss you?
You kidding? My dad couldn't wait to see the back of me.

But surely your mom ...?
Mom's dead. But don't worry about it, I barely knew her.

Right, right. OK, you seem like perfect Last Stop employee material, but there's one more thing. There's a lot of heavy lifting involved with the job, and I need to see if you can handle it.
Coffee Corner

Totally, man. I can lift amps all day. I'm really strong.

STAFF ONLY
Coffee Corner
I'll bet. Here, come with me into the basement and help me bring some cases of beer up.

Sure! Do I get to keep any?
Hey, it was just a joke! Why are you looking at me like that?

What the hell are you doing? What the ...
Aaaaaaugh!!!!

Coffee Corner
Kid ... you're hired.

ACKNOWLEDGEMENTS

Jessica ABEL

Life Sucks has a long history, and owes its existence to the help and encouragement of many people. Most particularly, I want to thank my partner Gabe for his fantastic ability to spin out tales from the paltriest of beer-soaked sparks, and for his willingness to then run those tales through the wringer with me and build them into the story you hold in your hands. I also especially want to thank Warren, whom we held prisoner at his drawing board for more than a year while he elegantly and faithfully brought the characters and world of *Life Sucks* into full-fleshed being.

Back when *Life Sucks* was called "Night Shift", there was a small group of people who helped us make the leap to the next stage: Ken Levin contributed crucial editorial feedback (and possibly the title!) and contract-making acumen, and Thomas Ragon's enthusiasm kept us on track.

In its final incarnation, *Life Sucks* has had the input and labor of a whole team of talented people. My thanks go to Mark Siegel for his editorial vision, Tanya McKinnon for her clear reading, Hilary Sycamore for her lovely coloring (and infinite patience with my picky comments), and Danica Novgorodoff, Kat Kopit, Craig Owen, Einav Aviram, and Greg Stadnyk for being such consummate professionals, and for their invaluable contributions to making this project the best possible version of itself.

Finally, I thank Matt for his unwavering interest in this book and his support during the process of creating it. Not to mention for his one-third share of germ of the idea back on February 24, 2002—and the Palm Pilot that enshrined it.

Gabe SORIA

First off, this project would be pointless if I couldn't share its completion with my lovely wife, Amanda, and our son, Caleb. You two give everything I do meaning.

Jessica Abel is a dynamo—a creative force of nature who also knows when to crack the whip over the head of a guy perpetually looking for an excuse not to work. Without her, this book would not exist. You couldn't ask for a better friend or collaborator.

I couldn't imagine this book with art by anybody but Warren Pleece. His enthusiasm, his eye

for detail, and his mind-boggling speed and seemingly effortless skill are extraordinary. He makes Jess and me look good. Really, he's a prince.

And in no particular order, I'd also like to thank: the Drunken Spacemen's Guild, Nick Bertozzi and family, Dean Haspiel, Paul Pope, Mark Siegel, Nikos Constant, St. John Frizell and Linden Elstran, Matt Madden, Alex Cox and Rocketship Comics, Mom, Dad, Lisa, Natalie and Caroline, Dan Auerbach, Patrick Carney, Matt and Madeleine, Pete Relic, Jay Babcock, Preston Long, Steve Burns, Brent Rollins, Paul Cullum, John Patterson, Sean Howe, Alex Pappademas, Andy Bizer, Bailey Smith, Andrew Knowlton, Christina Skogly, Wade Hammett and family, Chris Cummings, Robert Starnes, Deliverators, Jon Seder, Steve Thomas and More Fun Comics, Gaston Dominguez-Letelier, Ilia Letelier and Meltdown Comics, Morgan Night, Ian Wheeler-Nicholson, Annie Wedekind, David Teague, Scott Adkins at the Brooklyn Writer's Space, Michael Wright, Rob Semmer, and the extended Soria and Bingham families in Redlands and Los Angeles.

Warren PLEECE

Many thanks to Nick Abadzis, who pointed me in the right direction, Jessica and Gabe for letting me come along for the ride and for all their encouragement and enthusiasm, and Mark Siegel and the rest of the First Second team for their patience and peachy keenness.

Also, I'd like to thank Hilary Sycamore for breathing some life into the black and white, to Craig Owen for making a font from my scrawl, and to Janet Ginsburg for the LA photos.

Finally, a big thank you to my boys, Frank and Georgy, who got to see all of this first and to my wife, Sue Currell, who kept us all going and got us through to the other side.

New York & London

Published by First Second
First Second is an imprint of Roaring Brook Press,
a division of Holtzbrinck Publishing Holdings Limited Partnership
175 Fifth Avenue, New York, NY 10010

Distributed in Canada by H. B. Fenn and Company Ltd.
Distributed in the United Kingdom by Macmillan Children's Books, a division of Pan Macmillan.

Design by Einav Aviram and Danica Novgorodoff

Library of Congress Cataloging-in-Publication Data

Abel, Jessica.
Life sucks / text by Jessica Abel and Gabriel Soria ; art by Warren Pleece ; coloring by Hilary Sycamore. -- 1st American ed.
p. cm.
ISBN-13: 978-1-59643-107-2
ISBN-10: 1-59643-107-5
1. Graphic novels. I. Soria, Gabriel. II. Pleece, Warren. III. Title.
PN6727.A25L54 2008
741.5'973--dc22
2006102546

COLLECTOR'S EDITION
ISBN-13: 978-1-59643-364-9
ISBN-10: 1-59643-364-7

First Second books are available for special promotions and premiums.
For details, contact: Director of Special Markets, Holtzbrinck Publishers.

First Edition May 2008
Printed in China

1 3 5 7 9 10 8 6 4 2